THE GREAT MIGUEL

Gretchel P. Paculaba

ISBN
Hardbound-978-621-495-279-3
Softbound/Paperback- 978-621-495-280-9
Mobile/Kindle- 978-621-495-281-6

Published by:
Poetry Planet Book Publishing House
Rosario, Pozorrubio, Pangasinan, Philippines
Contact Number:075-6155455
Email: maritesritumalta@gmail.com

PREFACE

Reading storybook is a powerful tool that can enrich our lives in countless ways. By immersing ourselves in the worlds of others, we can expand our horizons, deepen our understanding of the world, and cultivate a lifelong love of learning. That's why I write this story book titled "The Great Miguel".

The story is about a young boy named Miguel who discovers that greatness comes in many forms. Join him on an exciting adventure filled with friendship, courage, and the magic of believing in oneself.

In this book, you will see how Miguel faces challenges, makes new friends, and learns important lessons about kindness and bravery. Through his journey, he shows us that being great isn't just about being the best; it's about being true to yourself and helping others along the way.

I hope you enjoy reading about Miguel's adventures as much as I enjoyed writing them. Remember, each of you has the power to be great in your own unique way!

Happy reading!

The Author

In a distant field in Siacan, there was a young boy named Miguel. His life was full of hardships. His parents were only farmers, and their income was not enough to feed their family. Despite life challenges, Miguel is a kind and helpful child who is willing to do anything to help his parents.

One day, while he was looking for fresh nuts in the farm. At a glance, he saw a group of young boys walking on their farm carrying garbage, without hesitation, dumped it in their farm. There were also people cutting down trees, which could lead to slight deforestation in their area, making it unsafe for children and animals.

Miguel realizes and thinks about what ways he could get rid of the trash in their area. As a consequence of his determination, Miguel made the choice to fight. He supported the community's advocacy in organizing a large platform in their community to clean surroundings, rivers, and take action on tree planting.

Miguel realizes and thinks about what ways he could get rid of the trash in their area. As a consequence of his determination, Miguel made the choice to fight. He supported the community's advocacy in organizing a large platform in their community to clean surroundings, rivers, and take action on tree planting.

They encouraged the community's elders and young people to cooperate in order to accomplish their objective. Everyone is driven to support one another. Thus, they began cleaning up the surroundings and planting trees.

Miguel was glad to support his fellow neighbors for their advocacy. The young people continued to maintain the cleaning and greening initiatives. They gradually restore the beauty of their surroundings with the support of the youth in their community. As a result of the area's steady cleaning.

Sadly, there was a conflict in the area since some adults didn't agree with the local barrio's cleaning and greening project priority. Many adults believed that the best way to escape poverty was to work hard and gain money rather than helping to clean up the environment. For them, working so hard without a reliable source of income to enhance their everyday lives is a waste of a better chance to raise their socioeconomic standing.

The time came, the community was divided into two groups: those who favored Miguel's project and those who felt the opposite. The conflict in each other's views has caused barriers throughout the community. However, Miguel’s group gave time and patience to advocate their desire for a clean environment. Moreover, there are residents who are worried about how it will affect their respective sources of income.

In spite of problem arise, Miguel and his companions did not miss hope. Their efforts to persuade the young people in their neighborhood to embrace the clean-up campaign are currently ongoing.

With sustained efforts and support from the community's youth, they gradually come to see the program's worth and the significance of their advocacy. They realized that some members of the community, whose goal was not only for them but for the future of the next generation.

Eventually, they achieved their goal. With the help of the entire community, they restored the beauty of their forest, and their place became the role model for the entire town. All residents learned that by working together, not just for their own lives and the lives of others, but for all living.

ABOUT THE AUTHOR

GRETCHEL PLAZOS PACULABA, the author, currently teaches at Mangilay II Elementary School in Mangilay, Siayan, Zamboanga Del Norte as a Teacher III. She was born on December 14, 1992. She graduated with a Bachelor of Elementary Education, major in General Education, and a Master of Arts in Education, major in Educational Administration at J.H. Cerilles State College – Dumingag Campus, Dumingag, Zamboanga del Sur.

She is a dedicated second-grade teacher and a former school reading coordinator, leaving a deep impact on the lives of her learners. Over the past five years, she has inspired many children to love reading. Her experience as a school reading coordinator has given her a broader perspective on the importance of reading. She has come to understand how reading can significantly influence a child's development. This understanding has intensified her desire to contribute to the growth of young readers.

The publication of this book is historic for the author as it is her first children's book aimed at educating children across the country, particularly those in the second grade. This is a wonderful opportunity for the author to share her creativity and leave a positive impression on the lives of children. It is a way to provide enjoyment, knowledge, and inspiration to future generations of readers.

www.ingramcontent.com/pod-product-compliance
Lightning Source LLC
LaVergne TN
LVHW071116160826
845679LV00004B/1091
9786214952809